Bounce Alert in Toy Town

Collins

It was a sunny morning in Toy Town...

Everything was peaceful.
   Noddy smiled to himself. "I wonder what's happening in Toy Town today?"

At Dinah Doll's stall the two goblins, Sly and Gobbo, were up to their usual tricks.

"We'll pay you on Friday," said Gobbo, grinning slyly. "Promise!"

"I never believe what goblins say when they have their fingers crossed," said Dinah. "It means they're not telling the truth!"

"Fingers crossed?" said Gobbo, pretending to be amazed. "Now how did that happen?"

Noddy chuckled to see Dinah Doll outsmart the
two cheating goblins.

"Good old Toy Town," he said with a happy sigh.
"Nice and calm as usual."

Wheeeet-wheeeet-wheeeet!

Noddy spun around.

Mr Plod the policeman was blowing his whistle. There was an emergency! What was going on? Mr Plod was running through the streets shouting, "Bounce alert! Bounce alert!"

Dinah quickly closed up her stall, and Noddy gasped in surprise to see everyone in Toy Town running inside their houses and shutting all their doors and windows.

"What ever is a bounce alert?" he wondered, getting more and more bewildered.

"You'd better get inside, Noddy," warned Dinah Doll. "They can get very rowdy sometimes!"

"*Who* can get rowdy sometimes?" Noddy called after her, but Dinah raced into Mr Sparks' garage and quickly pulled down the green roller door.

Big-Ears was reading outside, but he quickly ran indoors.

Even the goblins were trying to find somewhere to hide. Gobbo banged on the door, yelling, "Let us in, Big-Ears. We promise not to eat all the ice cream, this time!"

"Please! They're coming!" shrieked Sly.
Big-Ears' muffled voice came through the door,
"Your fingers are crossed! And we all know
what *that* means."

"Drat," said Gobbo. "Come on, Sly, we've
got to hide."

The goblins ran off as fast as they could
towards Town Square.

Boing!... Boing!... Boing!... Boing!...

"What ever is that noise?" said Noddy, looking all around him. Then he saw.

"Wow! Look at those balls bounce!"

Boing!... Boing!... Boing!...
   Blue balls, green balls, pink balls, stripy balls.
They were having a wonderful time bouncing
all over Toy Town.
   Boing!... Boing!... Boing!... Boing!...
   Noddy loved them. "Yippeeee!" he yelled.

But one little blue ball just couldn't bounce as high as the others.

The big balls glared angrily at the little one and he looked sad.

Spoing!… spoing!… spoing!

The little blue ball plopped away by himself and came to a halt beside Noddy.

"Don't worry," said Noddy, kindly. "You're smaller than the others, but that's OK. I'm small too! I'll call you Tiny."

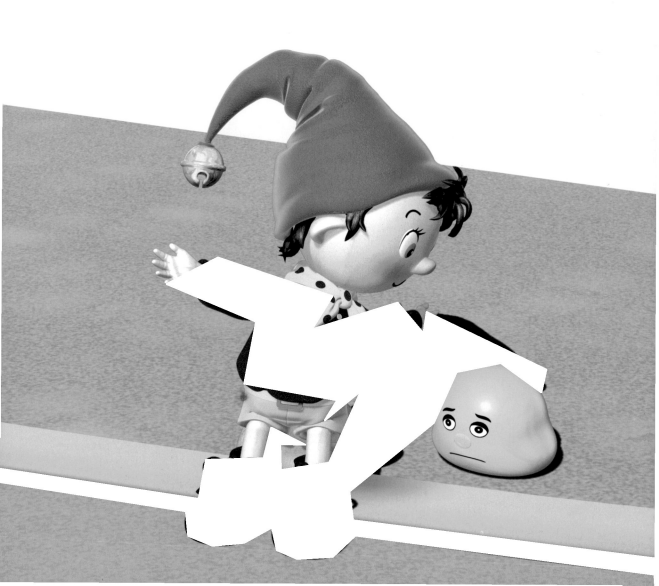

Noddy picked up the little blue ball and sang
a song to cheer him up:

> When you are small, life isn't all bad,
> When you are small, you should be glad.
> Yes, take it from me, tiny blue ball,
> You ought to be glad you are small.

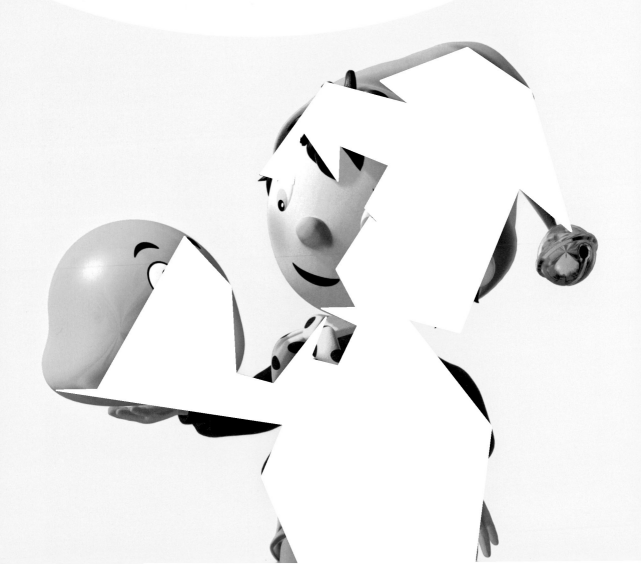

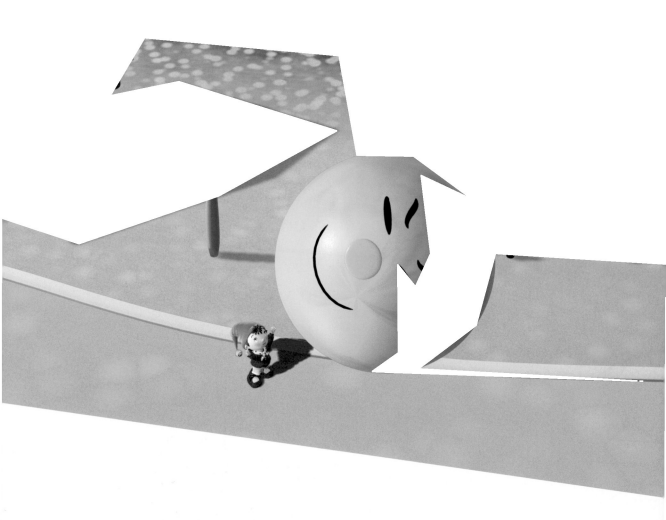

"Hey, Tiny! I know a game you'll like," said Noddy, picking up the little blue ball and throwing him as high as he could into the air.

Wheeeeeeee! The little blue ball grinned happily.

"You like that, don't you?" said Noddy, throwing him high into the air again and again.

Meanwhile, the other Bouncy Balls had found the goblins in Town Square.

"Hey, you Bouncy Balls have too much fun," yelled Gobbo.

"We don't like it when anyone else has fun – only when we do," said Sly.

"Yeah. So buzz off," said Gobbo.

The Bouncy Balls bounced a little closer…

"Run!" Gobbo shrieked, running off as fast as he could.

Sly followed him.

The Bouncy Balls were delighted. Squeaking gleefully, they bounced after the two goblins and chased them all the way out of Toy Town.

At last Sly and Gobbo managed to escape.

"Those rotten Bouncy Balls," moaned Sly. "They keep picking on us."

"We've got to get rid of them for good," said Gobbo. "Listen, I've got a plan – but first we need a big net…"

A little later, Gobbo and Sly had their trap ready.
  "Come over here, Bouncy Balls!" called Sly.
  "We've got a surprise for you!" sniggered Gobbo.
  The Bouncy Balls rushed after them to see what
the surprise was. But Gobbo wouldn't say any more
until all the Bouncy Balls had gathered together,
even the little blue ball.

"OK… Now PULL, Sly!" Gobbo yelled. "HARD!"

The trap worked. Sly pulled hard on a rope and WHOOSH! All the Bouncy Balls were whisked up in a net.

"Ha-ha-ha!" Gobbo giggled as the two goblins ran away. "That's where you're going to stay, you Bouncy Balls, hanging up in the air! You'll never bother us again with your silly bouncing."

But he was wrong. Only one ball could save the Bouncy Balls now. The brave little blue ball was just small enough to squeeze through the holes in the net.

SPOING!

And he bounced as fast as he could, all the way back to Toy Town to get help.

Ploink... Ploink... Ploink... Ploink...

The little blue ball went straight to Noddy's car
and bounced on it.

"Hi, Tiny. What's wrong?" asked Noddy. The
little blue ball looked anxious and bounced again.
SPOING!

Noddy was worried. "We'd better get Mr Plod.
He's the best help there is when there's trouble."

"This had better not be some Bouncy Ball trick," said Mr Plod as they drove out of Toy Town.

"Tiny wouldn't play a trick on us, Mr Plod," said Noddy. "I'm sure the Bouncy Balls are in trouble."

"Uh-oh!" gasped Noddy, "LOOK!"

There were the Bouncy Balls, dangling in a net from a high branch of a tree.

"*Squeak-squeak-squeak!*" they cried.

"Hm. This looks like a nasty goblin trick," said Mr Plod as he untied the rope and set the Bouncy Balls free.

BOING!... BOING!... BOING!... BOING!

"You saved them, Tiny," Noddy told the little blue ball.

Then Noddy took a bicycle pump out of his car. "I almost forgot. Mr Sparks lent me this for you." He added, "Soon you'll be able to bounce as high as the other Bouncy Balls!"

When the little blue ball was properly pumped up he could bounce HIGHER than any of the others. "Wow!" Noddy laughed as the blue ball shot into the air. "Maybe I should call you Sky Rocket from now on!"

Just then, Sly and Gobbo came back to gloat.

"We're coming to laugh at you – you never-bounce-again Bouncy Balls," sneered Gobbo.

"Yeah! Feeling all strung up, are you?" sniggered Sly.

"Aghh!" they both gasped.

The balls had gone! But there was Noddy and Mr Plod, waiting for them!

"Tricking the Bouncy Balls was a very bad thing to do," said Mr Plod. "But I'm not going to put you in jail –"

The two goblins grinned.

Mr Plod went on, "– I'm going to leave you to the Bouncy Balls!"

"Oh, no!" shrieked the goblins, and they ran off as fast as they could.

First published in Great Britain by HarperCollins Publishers Ltd in 2002

5 7 9 10 8 6 4

This edition published by HarperCollins Children's Books
HarperCollins Children's Books is a division of HarperCollins Publishers Ltd.

ISBN: 0 00 715103 9

A CIP catalogue for this title is available from the British Library.

Printed and bound by Printing Express Ltd., Hong Kong

make way for NODDY™

Collect them all!

Do-It-Yourself Noddy
ISBN 0 00 712241 1

Noddy Goes Shopping
ISBN 0 00 712242 X

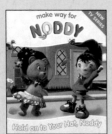

Hold on to your Hat, Noddy
ISBN 0 00 712243 8

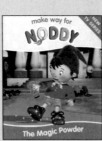

The Magic Powder
ISBN 0 00 715101 2

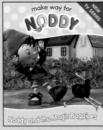

Noddy and the Magic Bagpipes
ISBN 0 00 712366 3

Noddy and the New Taxi
ISBN 0 00 712239 X

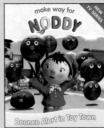

Bounce Alert in Toy Town
ISBN 0 00 715103 9

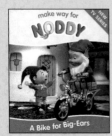

A Bike for Big-Ears
ISBN 0 00 715105 5

Noddy's Perfect Gift
ISBN 0 00 712365 5

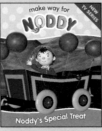

Noddy's Special Treat
ISBN 0 00 712362 0

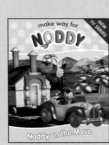

Noddy on the Move
ISBN 0 00 715678 2

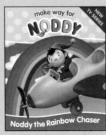

Noddy the Rainbow Chaser
ISBN 0 00 715677 4

And send off for your free Noddy poster (rrp £3.99).
Simply collect 4 tokens and complete the coupon below.

TOKEN

Name: _____

Address: _____

_____

_____

e-mail: _____

❏ Tick here if you do wish to receive further information about children's books.

Send coupon to: **Noddy Poster Offer, PO Box 142, Horsham, RH13 5FJ**

Terms and conditions: proof of sending cannot be considered proof of receipt. Not redeemable for cash. 28 days delivery.
Offer open to UK residents only.

UNIVERSAL

Make Way for Noddy videos now available at all good retailers